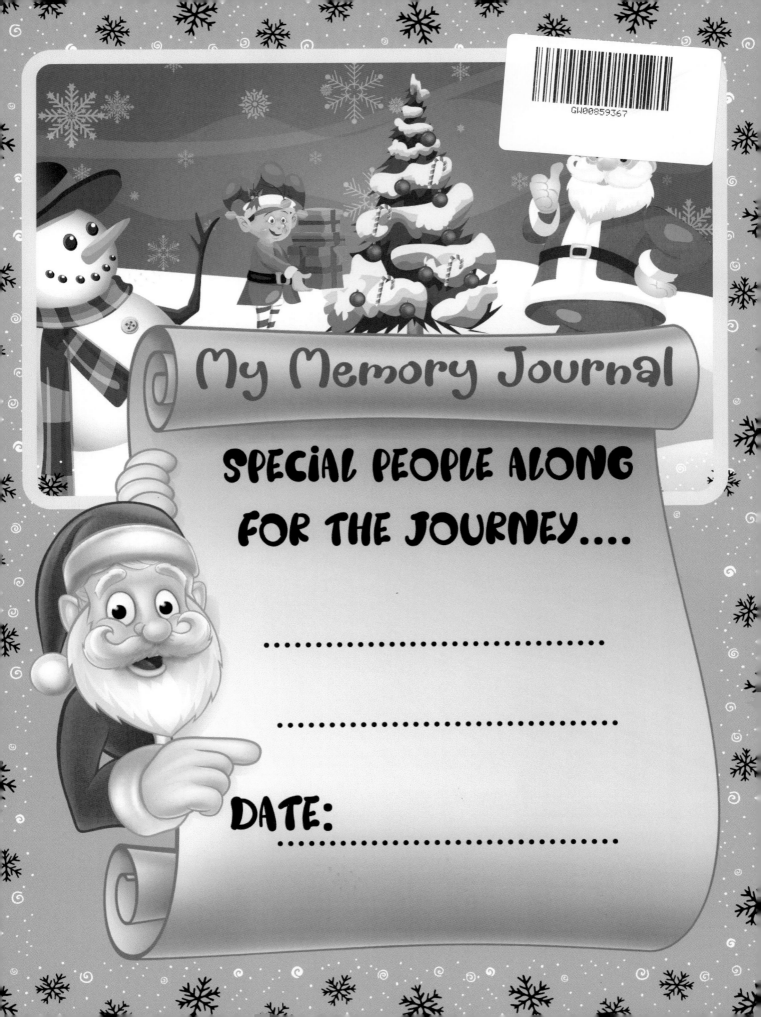

# My Memory Journal

## SPECIAL PEOPLE ALONG FOR THE JOURNEY....

..............................................

..............................................

DATE:
..............................................

THE BEST THING ABOUT Memories IS MAKING THEM

The greatest gift you can give your child is time with you!

This journal is designed as a keepsake of your precious time together.

The beauty of your journal, is that it can be gifted to your child or another family member who may not be near this Chrristmas.

# ADVENT ADVENTURE

# DAY 1

Why not talk to your child about your
favourite childhood Christmas memories.
Ask older siblings about theirs too.
Now's the time to dig out Christmas jumpers and pyjamas.
Why not put the Christmas pyjamas at the end of the bed for tonight.
Your children will be surprised when
they see them!

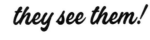

ADVENT ADVENTURE

Lovely Memories

Write some of your thoughts......

........................................

........................................

........................................

Perhaps start some new traditions......

Thoughts &
Ideas

Thoughts &
Ideas

# Welly-up for a Winterwalk

Go for a Winter walk and be in the moment. Think about what was the weather like? **What have you seen?**

Collect pinecones, twigs to make decorations tomorrow

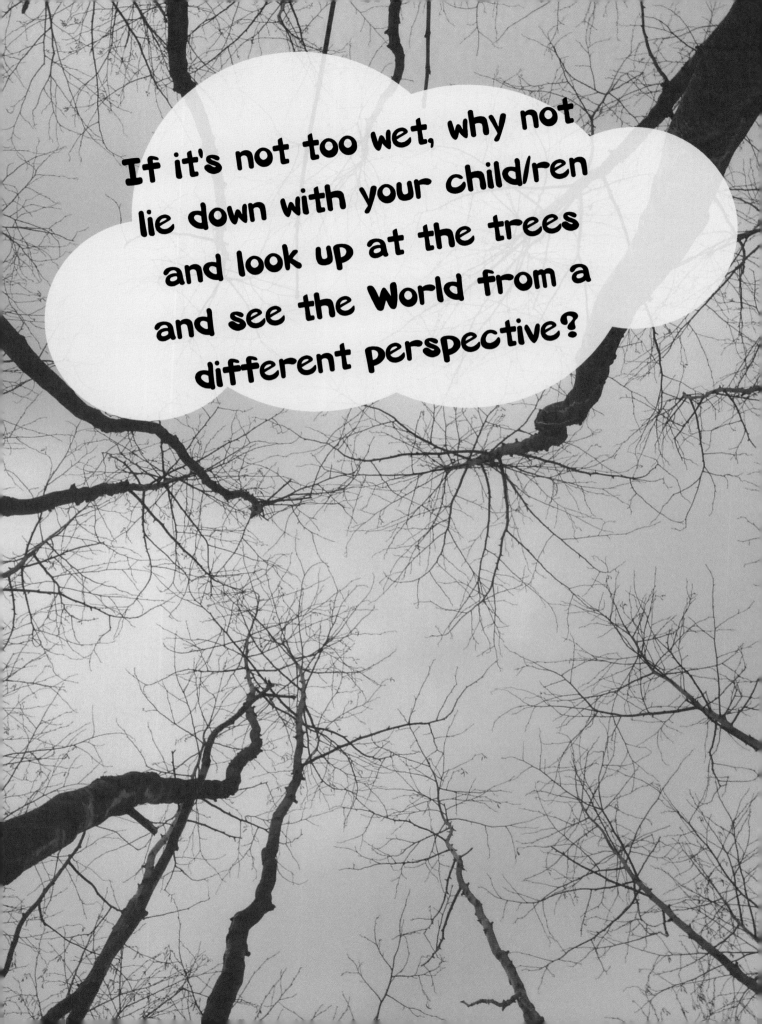

# Welly-up Checklist

## What did you see/find?

- [ ] ................................................................
- [ ] ................................................................
- [ ] ................................................................
- [ ] ................................................................
- [ ] ................................................................
- [ ] ................................................................
- [ ] ................................................................
- [ ] ................................................................
- [ ] ................................................................
- [ ] ................................................................

- [ ] ................................................................
- [ ] ................................................................
- [ ] ................................................................
- [ ] ................................................................
- [ ] ................................................................
- [ ] ................................................................
- [ ] ................................................................
- [ ] ................................................................
- [ ] ................................................................
- [ ] ................................................................

Photo here

Christmas Crafting

Day 3

Create a Christmas card or a simple decoration using some of your finds on your walk

Use some dried orange and spices to add magical Christmas smells.

Happy Holidays!

# Christmas Crafting

What did you make?

Place a sample or photograph

here:

# As an additional activity, you may like to copy this page or cut it out and help your child/ren to write on them

 As an additional activity, you may like to copy this page or cut it out and help your child/ren to write on them

*Thoughts &*
*Ideas*

# Letter to Santa

**Day 4**

ASK YOUR CHILD/REN TO WRITE A CHRISTMAS LETTER TO SANTA ABOUT WHAT THEY'VE DONE THIS YEAR (USE THE LETTRR TEMPLATES IF YOU PREFER).

ASK YOUR CHILD/REN TO DRAW WHAT THEY'D LIKE AND WHAT THEY'D LIKE TO DO WITH YOU NEXT YEAR

PERHAPS YOU COULD MAKE VOUCHERS OR IOU'S FOR ACTIVITIES, SUCH AS COOKING OR PLAYING A GAME WITH THEM.

In the UK, you can send your letter for free via Royal Mail free until 10th December 2021. Send to:

**Santa/Father Christmas,
Santas Grotto,
Reindeer Land, XM4 5HQ**

https://www.royalmail.com/christmas/letters-to-santa

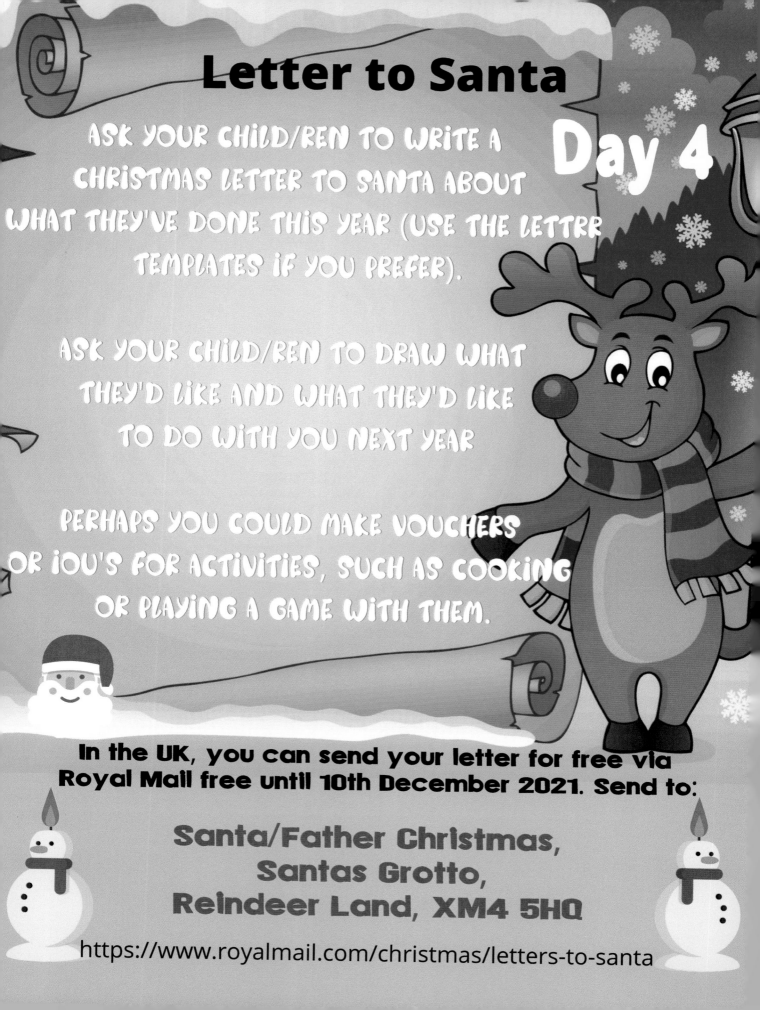

# Dear Santa

★ ★ ★ ★ ★ ★ ★ ★ ★ ★ ★

MY NAME IS .............................................................

☐ GIRL   ☐ BOY   I AM ......... YEARS OLD.

I want to ask you .........................................

.................................................................................

.................................................................................

## • THIS IS MY •
## CHRISTMAS
### ★ LIST ★

🎁 ....................................

.................................................

.................................................

.................................................

.................................................

### I DREW THIS FOR YOU.

Love,

.................................................

# I will leave
### YOU SOME COOKIES AND MILK!

# Dear Little Friend

★ ★ ★ ★ ★

...................................................................

...................................................................

...................................................................

...................................................................

...................................................................

...................................................................

...................................................................

NAUGHTY ☐ NICE ☐

Santa
★ ★ ★ ★ ★ ★ ★
CLAUS

OFFICIAL SEAL OF THE
Santa
★ NORTH POLE ★

# SING A LONG A CAROL

# DAY 5

PLAY THE RADIO IN THE CAR AND SING ALONG TO CHRISTMAS SONGS WITH YOUR CHILD/REN. LISTEN TO YOUR CHILD/REN SING NEW SONGS LEARNED AT NURSERY/SCHOOL.

# Spread the love - Kindness
## Donate a toy your child has grown out of

Day 7

# We see you!

## Day 8

**Have a Virtual party/Whatsapp/Facetime chat with those family or friends who you may not see this Year**

*Thoughts &*
*Ideas*

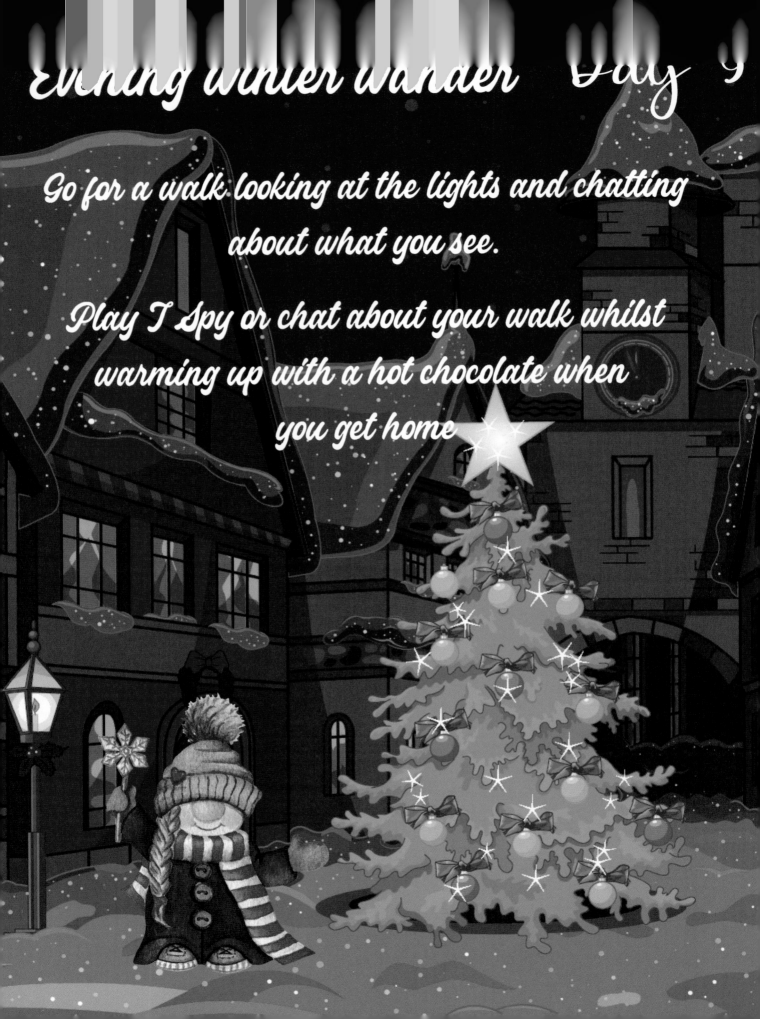

# Evening Winter Wander    Day 9

Go for a walk looking at the lights and chatting about what you see.

Play I Spy or chat about your walk whilst warming up with a hot chocolate when you get home

# CHRISTMAS I SPY

Put on some joyful music and Dance
around the kitchen, the lounge,
the bedroom.
Get your bodies moving and grooving!

Children laugh around 400 times a day, while the average is just 14 for adults! Get in touch with your inner child and share some laughter.

Tell your child/ren a joke, such as

Q: What kind of photos do elves take?

A: Elfies!

Or

Q: What do you call a cat sitting on the beach on Christmas Eve?

A: Sandy Claws!! They will love you for it..........

# Photo here

*Perhaps make this an annual tradition – see how much your child has grown*

# Love your library

Libraries are not just for lending,
but look out for free story times,
craft activities and competitions.
Why not borrow the
'Night before Christmas'
to read on Christmas Eve

# Snuggle up a Story   Day 15

Snuggle up with a story at bedtime from a book chosen from the library or from school

Children love finding things and this activity is a great conversation starter

# Christmas
## Scavenger Hunt

Tree ☐

Ornament ☐

Gift ☐

Santa ☐

Wreath ☐

Lights ☐

Stocking ☐

Snowman ☐

Holly ☐

Candy Cane ☐

Plus the fresh air and exercise will aid sleep at this exciting time of year!

# THOUGHTS & IDEAS

Day 17

## Spread a Little Cheer

Encourage your child/ren to say thank you to their teacher/nursery worker

Joy

Draw a picture or give a card

THANK YOU
for helping me
GROW

Learn to say thank you in sign language –
extend the activity by learning Happy Christmas too!

**1**

**2**

Your flat hand goes outward
and away from your chin.

thank you

Day 18
Elf yourself

Elf has left you this Christmas cookie recipe, but as you know he's a bit mischievous so the ingredients are not where you'd expect them to be! Can your child/ren find where you've hidden them?

Flour ALL-PURPOSE 1KG

BAKING SODA

SUGAR

SWEET Sugar PURE GRANULATED 2KG

# CHRISTMAS COOKIE COOKING

Make some Christmas cookie cooking
(don't forget to make extra for gifts)

## Ingredients

350g/12¼oz plain flour, 1 tsp bicarbonate of soda,
1 tsp salt, 225g/8oz butter, 175g/6¼oz caster sugar,
175g/6¼oz soft brown sugar1 tsp vanilla extract.
2 free-range eggs,
350g/12¼oz dark chocolate crumbled or chocolate chips

## Method

Preheat the oven to 190C/375F/Gas 5.
In a bowl, combine the flour, baking soda and salt. In another bowl,
combine the butter, sugar, brown sugar and vanilla extract until creamy.
Beat in the eggs. Gradually beat in the flour mixture. Stir in the chocolate.

Split the pliable dough into two halves, rolling each out into sausage shapes,
approximately 5cm/2in in diameter. Wrap them in cling film
and transfer to the refrigerator until ready to use.

When you are ready to bake the cookies, simply cut the log
into slices 2cm/¾in thick and lay on a baking tray, widely
spaced apart.
Bake for 9-11 minutes until just golden-brown on the edges.
Allow to cool for a few minutes on the tray before
transferring to a wire rack.
Enjoy warm with a glass of
ice cold milk.

# Thoughts & Recipe Ideas

Peace

# The Speedy Snowman

Set out a selection of clothes that are suitable for a snowman for example, a scarf or gloves. Ask the child to collect a piece of clothing, run back to you and put it on.
Race against their own time or siblings.

Add a photograph here!

*Thoughts &*
*Ideas*

# Hum the Hymn Day 21

**Hum a well known hymn, carol or song that your child would know and see if they can guess what it is!**

God Rest You Merry, Gentlemen    O Tannenbaum

Go Tell It on the Mountain

The First Noel    DECK THE HALLS    Carol of the Bells    We Three Kings

O Come, All Ye Faithful    I Heard the Bells on Christmas Day

Oh Christmas Tree    Silent Night

O Little Town of Bethlehem    All I want For Christmas is You

HARK! THE HERALD ANGELS SING

ITS THE MOST WONDERFUL TIME OF THE YEAR

Away in a Manger    The Little Drummer Boy

Angels we have heard on high

I'll Be Home for Christmas    Rockin' Around the Christmas Tree

Jingle Bells    Let it Snow!

Do You Hear What I Hear?    SILVER BELLS

O Come, O Come, Emmanuel

Joy to the World    The Holy Boy

I Come with Love    Santa Claus is Coming to Town

SLEIGH RIDE

Blue Christmas    Have Yourself a Merry Little Christmas

It Came Upon the Midnight Clear    WHITE CHRISTMAS

I HEARD THE BELLS ON CHRISTMAS DAY

What Child Is This?    We Wish You a Merry Christmas

GIGGLY GAMES NIGHT

Day 22

TODAY PLAY SOME OF YOUR FAMILY FAVOURITES -
MUSICAL BUMPS, MUSICAL STATUES, MUSICAL CHAIRS,
OR A MEMORY GAME. PLACE ITEMS ON A TRAY AND TAKE ONE AWAY-
CHILD HAS TO GUESS WHAT'S GONE

# Movie Marathon

Snuggle up to watch your favourite Christmas films

MOVIE

MOVIE NIGHT

# Read the 'Night before Christmas' before hanging up the stocking/s and watch a Santa Tracker

Day 24

MAY YOU NEVER BE TOO OLD
TO SEARCH THE SKIES ON

*Christmas Eve*

Thoughts &
Ideas

# Enjoy the day - you deserve it!

## Day 25

# MERRY CHRISTMAS!

You have filled the Holiday with endless traditions and memories.

You have taken precious moments that you have shared and kept them in your heart.

Your time is the greatest gift you can ever give your child/ren.

# Thoughts & Ideas

# Thoughts & Ideas

Printed in Great Britain
by Amazon